Grandma's Silent Auction
October
BY: Michael James

Copyright © 2020 by MICHAEL JAMES

All rights reserved.

No part of this book may be reproduced in any form or by any electronic or mechanical means, including information storage and retrieval systems, without written permission from the author, except for the use of brief quotations in a book review.

CHAPTER ONE
CIARA

Meeting Wyatt is one of the greatest things that has ever happened to me. I have learned so much about myself in the last month thanks to him. It's hard to believe that our time together ended this morning. It made me sad having to say goodbye to him and my heart hurts knowing he is gone. If someone told me back in August I'd fall in love with my bodyguard, I would have laughed in their face. I would have been the fool getting laughed at in return because I did fall in love with Wyatt. If Wyatt was the only guy I had feelings for, I wouldn't have let him leave without me. He made such an impact on my life.

My heart is being pulled in so many directions, I might not have one left to give to anyone. I couldn't be happier knowing I'm down to the last guy. I cannot tell myself to keep feelings out of this next relationship because it hasn't worked out so well for me in the last nine months. It would be wishful thinking if I wished Adler Vaughn was a complete asshole. I've learned Grams has very good taste when it comes to finding me a suitable husband. It makes me wonder why she never married herself. Why hasn't Grams found her one true love? If she has, she's never mentioned him to me. I understand Grams is a free spirit and she's always been an independent woman, but there has to be someone out there for her to love.

The beautiful October fall weather is setting in. Everything is so pretty in its fall colors. Alaska and I have been outside for her to get some playtime. She jumps on my legs for me to pick her up when Grams comes outside.

"Care to join me for lunch?"

"Actually, Grams, I'd love to."

"Wonderful. I can have Katie make us some sandwiches or we can dine out."

"Whichever you'd like."

"It's been a long time since we've been to Red Fox."

"Lunch and wine! Grams, I like where your head is."

"I'll meet you in the foyer once you have changed."

CHAPTER 1

"I'll be quick."

After I put Alaska in her kennel, then grab a change of clothing so that I can change really quick. When I get into the bathroom to freshen up, I see how my eyes are slightly swollen from crying when Wyatt left. I cried a lot saying goodbye to him. A huge part of me wished we didn't have to break up at all. I also wished Grams and him still thought I needed a bodyguard so that we didn't have to be apart.

Opening the top vanity drawer in the bathroom, I get some makeup out to conceal as much of my sadness as I can. Just as I'm about to apply the makeup, I wipe it off my finger. I'm upset and I don't care who sees it. I don't give a damn what others think of my appearance. My messy bun is staying put as well. I would change my clothes back to my sweats but I think Grams would have something to say about that.

The drive to Red Fox was a beautiful one. I love passing by the park to see all the colors the trees have sprung on us. I am not one to enjoy the cooler weather fall brings, but I do love seeing its display of art. I think Grams enjoyed the ride as well.

We were seated at a table near the windows and it doesn't take long for a server to take our order. If it weren't for a slight drizzle outdoors we would have sat outside. This spot is perfect for people watching. Since we know my mother was the one behind all the chaos in the past few months, I no longer need to worry about exposing myself in public. I told Grams about seeing my mother. She wasn't too thrilled that I did. She didn't calm down until she knew I wasn't alone, that Wyatt was with me and he wouldn't allow anything to happen to me. Grams and I had a long discussion about if we wanted to press charges or not. When all of this happened I was all for getting the person responsible, then I met her and felt sorry for her. Not sorry as in I felt compassion for her, sorry that she turned into such a pathetic person. There was no need for her to get money the way she did. She could have come to me or Grams like an adult. If Grams wouldn't have helped Cassidy, I would have. What it all boils down to is, she's still my mother. I don't want any ill feelings toward her. I don't want her to die. I also don't want anything from her. There will be no shared lunch or dinner as she asked. No relationship period. I didn't have her as a mother growing up and I don't want one now. Seeing her for who she is helped me get over the past. I realized in the few moments I did spend with Cassidy that she is toxic. If she were the one to raise me, who knows how my life would have turned out. I was better off without her.

"What is going through your mind?"

"I was thinking about how grateful I am that you raised me. Who knows where I'd be without you."

"You know I would never have let my daughter keep you away from me, right? I knew Cassy wasn't fit to be a parent and I would have fought to keep you if she tried taking you. Regardless of all that, you're a strong woman, Ciara. You would have turned out to be as amazing as you are all on your own."

"My gut is telling me she isn't sick with kidney failure."

"Your gut is right. After our discussion, I went to have a chat with my darling daughter. Cassy isn't sick at all. She was playing games with you to see if you'd show any sympathy for her."

"How do we know that she is done messing with my life then?"

"I took care of it."

"Do I even want to ask how?"

"I threatened to cut off her monthly allowance and press charges. Jail time didn't sit well with her."

The server brings our lunch and refills our glasses.

Grams eyes are on me as I take a bite of my turkey BLT wrap. I use my napkin to cover my mouth as I speak.

"What?"

"You are different, do you know that?"

I swallowed my food. *"Different how?"*

"I'm not sure. Maybe love has changed you. You just have a new glow to your complexion. I've been seeing it for a while now. Whoever you end up with, I hope it never leaves because it looks good on you."

Grams smiles and then takes a bite of her lunch. I don't have a clue what she means by having a glow. I don't see myself any differently when I look in the mirror. I do, however, feel differently about my outlook on love. Whoever I end up with, whether it be one of the ten men or not, I will not settle as I had when dating in the past. The new woman in me sees I deserve a man who doesn't put me on the back burner. The person I choose to spend my life with will walk beside me, not ten steps in front.

"Speaking of love, have you seen Gary again?"

"I have a few times. He travels a lot. As far as love goes, I think that is out of the question."

"Grams, the guy is smitten with you." She shrugs her shoulders. I take a sip of my wine. Setting my glass back on the table, I study her. I think she likes

him. *"Why are you holding back? You do know it's not too late for love, right?"*

"I'm getting too old for that stuff."

"You are not!"

"Gary and I had a short love affair a long time ago. That ship sailed already."

"So you once had feelings for him?"

"I did. We were younger. It was around the time your mother left and he was just starting his career. Our timing wasn't good."

"Seems to me fate is on your side. I think you should give it a shot before I auction you off to ten bachelors for charity." I cannot believe Grams just rolled her eyes at me. *"You think I don't know ten men that would love to bid on the fabulous Millie Verbank? Think again, Grams, because I do."* I don't, but she doesn't need to know that.

Her phone rings and her eyes get big. I try to peek to see who it is, but she snatches her phone from my view too quickly. I eat my lunch as she answers the call. Her voice is soft and sweet as she talks. I see her face light up. I raise my brows as she looks at me. She rolls her eyes again then gets up from the table and walks outside. I cross my fingers it's Gary who has put a smile on her face.

Lunch with Grams was much needed. I love spending time with her and have missed our monthly get together at Red Fox for wine and food. I did feel a bit guilty that I didn't fully share with her about my visit with my mother. She doesn't know Wyatt told me my father's name and that Cassidy confirmed it. It was probably the only lie she didn't tell me. I didn't tell Grams about it because I am unsure what I want to do with the information. I don't take searching out my father lightly. If I ever do decide to find him, I want to make sure I'm mentally prepared for it. I have lived my life not knowing anything about him for this long, waiting a little bit longer isn't going to harm me. I have enough on my plate right now with other men in my life, I just don't think it's the right time to add another person in the mix.

After lunch, I came back to Grams to pack for the next adventure. I'll be swept off to meet Adler Vaughn at his home here in the city. As usual, I don't know anything more about him. I'm trying to keep an open mind, however, I don't really want to develop any kind of love connection.

"Knock knock!"

CHAPTER 1

"Gee whiz, you scared the crap out of me, Porter." I literally just about jumped out of my skin. He always sneaks up on me. I swear he's the quietest walker on this earth.

"How is my girl doing today?"

"I'm good. How are you?"

He plops his ass down on my bed. *"Ugh, fine."*

I nudge his shoulder. *"What's the matter?"*

"I'm extremely happy for you, but damn I miss you being around."

"I know, I miss you as well. On the bright side all this is almost over."

"Until you make your decision and begin a new life."

"Porter, my future involves you - always! Me being with a man isn't going to change anything with our friendship."

"You say that now, but wait until you decide where you will live."

"I already told you if I leave I want you to come with me. I need you in my life."

"I need you as well."

"But?"

"Not sure I will want to relocate."

"Let's not think about that right now. We are best friends and we will figure everything out."

"Where are you going this time?"

"Not far actually. Just to the other side of the city."

"Good, maybe I can meet him."

"Maybe." He picks at the nonexistent lint on my comforter. Something else is bothering him. *"What else is on your mind?"*

"I met a few of these guys. I'm worried about your state of mind. I know you and you don't like hurting anyone. I just don't see how you are going to officially break up with nine amazing men. How in the world are you going to pick just one and be okay afterward?"

"I have thought about this more times than I can count on both hands. I have no idea how I am going to get through it. I assume my best friend will be a shoulder to cry on and help me figure everything out."

"Of course I'll be here when you need me. It doesn't make it any easier knowing your personality."

Porter opens his arms and I cuddle up next to him. Oddly, he actually needs this more than I do. Normally the shoe is on the other foot.

"Want to stay the night? We can pig out and watch movies."

"I thought you'd never ask."

CHAPTER 1

"Great! I'll order our favorite pizza to start the evening off right."

I go to reach for my phone, but he holds me in place. Pizza can wait a little longer. Right now, my best friend needs me.

CHAPTER TWO
CIARA

This morning I woke up ready to go off and meet Adler. Then I said goodbye to Porter and watched him leave with Alaska and then my heart wished I wasn't going anywhere. I wished I could just snap my fingers and October would be over with. I don't know any magic so that isn't going to happen. A girl can wish, though. I went to find Grams after Porter left. I wanted to tell her goodbye and that I love her. I only had twenty minutes before a car would arrive and take me across the city. When I found her out on the patio, she was wrapped in a fuzzy blanket taking in the morning sun. We only had a few minutes together, but it was enough time to say what needed to be said. She told me I only had to get through one more month. The truth is, I have longer than that. Yes I'll be done meeting and dating the men, but then comes the real breakups. After I do all that, I'll still have another decision to make. It does weigh heavily on my mind about having a December wedding. I don't know if rushing into a marriage is the right thing to do after spending ten months dating different men. I got in the car unsure about my future. Doubts set in that love is impossible at the end of all of this. I hate how my mind can flip flop on the drop of a dime. I know love is possible because I have found love in more than one person. The reality is, I am scared to choose who to spend the rest of my life with. What if I pick the right guy and he has changed his mind about me? Some of the ones I dated early on, it's very possible that will happen. I met Malcolm ten months ago. That is a long time to hold feelings for a person you aren't even with. Hawk, he's a wild spontaneous bachelor. If I choose him, he could tell me he didn't wait for me to come back. Then my whole future is pretty much fucked. What am I supposed to do then? Run to the next guy and say I'm so sorry I made a mistake? Yeah, that isn't going to happen. No person wants to be second best.

By the time I snap out of my thoughts and have stressed myself out completely, we arrive at Adler's. I tilt my head and glance out the car window. I see nothing but a glass structure. You can't even see the sky, the building is so tall. This place looks more like an office building versus a home. After living out in the country, I don't think I could live in a building that houses this many apartments or condos. I could handle an apartment like mine because it is still more private than this place would be.

The driver opens the back door and I get out. I take quite a few deep breaths before stepping toward the front entrance. The door is held open for me, and I am greeted by a lady. It's a relief this place is an office building.

"Welcome, Ms. Verbank." She holds out her hand for me to shake. *"I am Elizabeth Gardner. I work for Mr. Vaughn. I'll be taking you to his office."*

"Hello," I manage to squeak out. I sound like a nervous child who got sent to the principal's office.

Elizabeth leads us to a set of elevators. Once the door opens we get in and I notice she hit the number twenty-two. Of course, it's the top floor. Heaven forbid anyone has an office on the first level. I am glad I don't have a fear of heights because my fears would have been tested in the last nine months. It doesn't take long before we reach the twenty-second floor. I follow Elizabeth off the elevator into a large open space with a reception desk. The young man behind the desk perks up and smiles, welcoming me to Vaughn Media. I said, *"Thank you,"* as I passed

CHAPTER 2

him and continued to follow Elizabeth to an office. I assume it is Adler's office.

"Adler is running a bit behind from his morning rounds. He'll be with you as soon as he can. Please, make yourself comfortable."

"Thank you."

With that, she leaves me alone in this big office. I scan the space to get a feel for who Adler is and what he might do for a living. There are books everywhere neatly placed on display. I walk over to one shelf that covers an entire inner wall. I read the name on the books and they all have *A.V. Martin* written on the spine. There are so many. I reach up and run my fingers along the spines as I walk past all the novels. My hand falls from the books as I leave the wall shelving and go over to his desk. His desk is neat and practically bare. No framed photos of his family or anything personal at all. Besides knowing Adler is into media, he still remains a mystery to me. I give up on trying to figure out who he is and go over to the windows and look at the city I was raised in. I remember what Wyatt said about one cannot see the world if the view is blocked. Maybe that is why all these men must have the top floor offices. They don't let anything block their view of where they want to go. To be successful one cannot go in blindly, it must be a clear vision to get where you are going.

"Ms. Verbank, sorry to keep you waiting."

I turn and see a man in a light blue suit jacket with a matching tie that he wears with a black pair of jeans. He stands tall beside his desk. His demeanor screams confidence from a mile away. He has light brown hair kept in a clean cut. He has just a little bit of silver showing through near the temple area. I am not going to try and guess his age, but I think he might be the oldest man of all the ones I already dated.

"Mr. Vaughn, I am assuming?"

"The one and only." he winks with a charming smile. So much for him being an asshole right off the bat. *"I hope your ride here was pleasant!"*

It was anything but pleasant. Alone time tends to get my brain working on overdrive. *"It was fine."*

"I cleared my schedule for the month. We are free to go to my home whenever you are ready."

"I am ready whenever you are."

"Would you like a tour of my floor before we head out?"

"What is it that you do, Mr. Vaughn?"

"I don't know if you noticed all the books over there."

"I did."

"I wrote all of them."

"Oh, the name on the spine threw me off."

"It's a pen name, most authors use them."

"So you write books, are they romance?"

"Nothing screams romance more than a happy ever after, right? Some of my writing is dark, some are I want your tears on my pages, but all are in the romance category."

"Sorry to say, I don't read books. I don't really have the time even if I wanted to read one."

"We will have to change that."

"Is that the only thing you do here? Write and publish your books?"

"I also scout for new authors that have great stories to tell. My team reads them, they pass the good ones onto me. If I like it, I make the author an offer. Afterward, my editing team works with the author for a clean read. The rest is history after that."

"What if one of your team members read a book and didn't like it, but it's actually a great story?"

"I have nine readers, they all read the same books. The ones with the most likes get passed onto me."

"That is interesting."

"Would you like a tour or do you wanna get the hell out of here?"

"Tour please."

There he goes again with his charming smile and a wink. I have wondered in the past how much romance is in an author's life or if ninety-nine percent of their story is total bullshit and they are the complete opposite of what they write. I guess I have a month to find out.

CHAPTER THREE
ADLER

A year ago I was contacted by Millie Verbank and she asked me flat out if I would like to date her granddaughter for a month. I seriously thought she was joking. My curiosity got the best of me, so I asked why only a month? Then she told me about the charity she donates to every year. That is what got my interest, if I'm being totally honest. Millie proceeded to tell me all the rules on dating her granddaughter and showed me a picture of her. Ciara is beautiful, that's a given. I thought about it for about a minute before I told her my conditions. Millie was ecstatic that I was going to place a bid. I was thrilled that my conditions were met. I'm an author and think outside the box. My mind works nonstop and I figured out how this all would benefit me, especially if I don't get the girl. Once I walked into my office today and saw Ciara in person, all my ideas went out the window. I mean hell, her picture doesn't do her justice. She is absolutely breathtaking. The way the sun's rays came in the window and shone on her, it was like a picture saying a thousand words. I stood by for a few seconds just taking in her beauty before I spoke. I consider myself lucky to have the privilege to see if her outer looks match what lies inside. I have an entire month to figure that out.

I gave Ciara a tour of my floor after a brief talk. I rarely spend time here in the office building, but I try to make it as homey as I can for my employees. My reading team doesn't sit behind desks. I have cozy lounge chairs, snacks and a nice warm fireplace lit for them. My editing team has the same privileges if they want. It's important for my team to choose where they are most comfortable. The more they enjoy coming to work, the more quality I get out of them.

After the tour Elizabeth told me she had my car waiting for me out front. I generally don't have her do that for me. I am perfectly capable of walking to the parking garage to retrieve my car on my own. I thought it was a nice gesture, though.

My condo isn't that close to my office. I purposely didn't want my home and work space too close by one another. You can never be too careful when it comes to keeping distance between authors and reading fans. Readers have a tendency of wanting to find out everything they can about their favorite author. My business has many bestselling authors that came to us when others turned them down. I wasn't afraid to publish them when they were a newbie on the scene. It isn't that difficult for fans to figure out where Vaughn Media is located. For some reason fans think they'll get a glimpse of their author if they come to the office building. They don't know I never sign contracts there. Authors rarely show their faces once I take on their stories.

"Are we heading out of the city?"

Ciara is a soft spoken woman. Her voice is calm and soothing. I bet if I were to piss her off, she would have no problem changing her tone. I could be wrong. After all, I just met the girl. I have no intentions of finding out if I'm right.

"Not quite, we are almost there."

"Have you always lived here?"

"No, I grew up in Kentucky."

"What made you move here?"

"I came here to get a book published when I was eighteen. I was turned down by many companies. I felt like I needed to prove who I was, so I stayed. I worked my ass off at a local restaurant waiting tables while I wrote in my spare time. I saved as much money as I

could. After being here for a little over two years, I finally got a break. Someone actually wanted to publish my book, the same one that was turned down two years prior. I took every dime I made and started up my company. I wasn't about to wait another two years."

"Wow, I see it paid off for you."

"It did. I was dedicated to what I believed in."

"How many books do you have written?"

"I lost count a long time ago."

I pull into the parking garage of my condo building and park my car in my dedicated spot. We get out and head to the elevators.

"Wait, I need my suitcase."

"We aren't staying here," I tell her.

"What do you mean?"

"We have a flight to catch at four."

"Where are we going?"

"My home in Kentucky."

"Oh."

"I just need to grab a few things before we can go. We should have time to get a bite to eat if you are hungry."

"I think I'm fine."

I give Ciara a quick tour of my condo. I tell her to make herself at home while I pack a few things. I don't need much, just my important things like my electronics. I don't need clothing because I have a closet full at home as I do here. Having two wardrobes makes traveling much lighter and faster.

❦

Ciara is a woman who needs to process the things around her to feel comfortable. I couldn't help but notice at my office the way she examined the space around her. She did the same thing at my condo and is doing it now that we are on my private plane. I think it's a good quality to have. One cannot be too cautious when in a new environment. I would be a fool if I believed she wasn't trying to process me as well. I'm new to her as she is to me. I am listening, watching, and learning myself. Body language is a powerful source of information if you pay close enough attention.

I reach across the small table that separates us and cover her fidgety hands with mine. Her dark brown eyes peek at me through her lashes. I glance down at my hands holding hers.

"I sense you are nervous. What can I do to ease your mind?"

"I wish there was an answer to that. I'll be fine once we are in the air. Even better after we land."

"How about you close your eyes, take a deep breath in and exhale it slowly." She does what I said. *"Again, but this time after you exhale don't open your eyes. Just stay focused on my voice."* She nods her head yes. I wait for her exhale. *"What is your favorite season?"*

"Spring."

"It was an early spring morning when I walked into my office ready to get my day started. I couldn't believe my eyes when I saw her standing at the window. The sun was bright as it shined against the window. The sun's rays in all their glory cast a bright glow all around her. I stood back to admire the beauty before me. I watched her take in the warmth of the sun. She then put her hands on the windowsill, tilted her face upward, and closed her eyes to take in God's creations. I wanted to walk toward her and take her in my embrace, but I was paralyzed. All I could do was stand in place and stare. I was so captivated by her, everything else around me didn't exist. There could have been an emergency in the building and I wouldn't have known. When she picked her head up, her head slowly turned in my direction. She saw me out of the corner of her eye over her shoulder. Her

lips curled at the corners ever so lightly. I tried to take a step toward her, but my body wouldn't move. I was dying inside to touch her sun-kissed skin, to take in the scent of her perfume that day, but mostly, I just wanted to gaze into her eyes and have her see me for who I am. That didn't happen, though. Instead she rushed past me as if she were running from a fire. I wanted more than anything to tell her not to run. The words just didn't come fast enough. She was gone. When my body finally stopped betraying me, I was able to walk the rest of the way to my desk. It was there that I picked the Styrofoam coffee cup that my little ray of sunshine left for me. I was upset that she once again left out a word. I had to figure out a way to get her to run toward me instead of away from me."

We have been in the air for quite some time. I could have stopped telling Ciara a story a while ago, but much like the guy I was talking about, I couldn't stop myself from taking in the beauty before me.

"Wow! Why did you stop?"

"I didn't want you to fall asleep on me."

"Why would I do that? I wanted to know if he got the girl or not."

"Maybe I'll continue to tell the story another time and we'll both know."

"I'd like that."

"Would you like a drink?"

"Maybe just some water if you have it." I get out of my seat to get us a drink. *"Is a story always that easy for you?"*

"Ya, I guess. I just let my mind wander and see where it goes."

"You got my full attention. I would love to read something of yours."

"When we get to my place you can pick whichever one you'd like."

"Thank you."

Ciara and I engage in light conversation the rest of the flight. I try to get to know her, but she is holding back a little. I am excited to learn more about this woman. I just hope she decides to let me in enough so that I can know her on a deeper level.

CHAPTER FOUR
CIARA

The way that Adler distracted me on the flight was unreal. Even though my body didn't physically move, I felt myself sitting on the edge of my seat, wanting more of his story. I was slightly disappointed he didn't keep going. Don't get me wrong, our conversation was wonderful, but damn that story was enticing. He definitely left me wanting more.

We landed in Kentucky a little over a half hour ago. Adler had a car waiting for us when we landed to take us to his home. The ride to his home was gorgeous. All the colors of the trees were remarkably warm and just stunning. It seems fall is happening way too fast. When I was at Wyatt's, it was just starting to change. I bet it's absolutely beautiful there this month. I wish I could see it.

I was expecting Adler to have a huge house up on a hill or something like that. I was pleasantly surprised to see his home is a small cobblestone cottage. I will be shocked if there are more than two bedrooms because the place looks that small. It is a really cute place. It almost makes me think of something that would belong in a Hallmark Christmas movie.

We get out of the car, and there is a fresh chill in the air. You can definitely smell the scent of fall. You don't really get that in the city. The air is pretty much stale there. Adler gets our luggage from the trunk of the car. When he looks at me, I smile. Then I tell him I love his place, because I really do. I am feeling a little giddy inside. I cannot wait to see what is inside.

As soon as Adler unlocks the door, he opens it and turns on a light. Stepping inside, my eyes travel all around the space. It really is simple, cozy, and has a warm feeling to it. He brings our belongings inside.

"I'll get us a fire going. It will be warm in no time at all."

"It is so cute."

"Cute, huh? That's such a girly thing to say." He smiles and winks at me to let me know he's joking around.

"I bet all the ladies you have brought here have said the same thing."

"Maybe they would if that were to happen."

"Are you telling me I'm the first woman to be here?"

"I am. This is my private place. My condo is a different story, though."

"I'm glad to know you aren't making yourself out to be a saint."

He laughs at my joke. *"I am far from being a saint. Unless you are a virgin, you are not a saint yourself."*

"I am a virgin." He looks at me as if I have two heads. I can't hold back my laughter. He chuckles. *"If I were, would you try to corrupt me? Bring me over to the dark side?"*

"Nah, I'd respect your wishes and take a lot of showers."

"So if you are in the bathroom a lot, don't bother you; got it."

"Or do the sinful thing and join me."

"You, Mr. Vaughn, may be trouble."

"Depends on your definition of trouble."

I stick my tongue out at him. *"You have a month to figure that out."*

Adler gets things ready to start a fire while I browse around his home. I was wrong about his place. It's only a one bedroom home. The bedroom is very spacious with a walk-in closet. There is only one bathroom. It isn't connected to the bedroom, it's across the hallway. His kitchen, eating area, and living room is one open floor plan. I saw a tiny office at the back of the house that is shared with a sunroom. It is there that I saw out into the back yard. It's mostly wooded, but what little yard there is, there is a fire pit and outdoor furniture. Alder's home really is cozy. I wonder why he's never brought a woman here before? What makes me so special to be the first? I have a lot to learn about this gorgeous man. He seems a bit mysterious to me, which is very intriguing.

I unpacked my suitcase. Adler was sweet enough to give me closet space. Once I was settled in and Alder got the house warmed, he asked me if I would like to go out to dinner. I told him it was too nice and cozy in the house to go out. He seemed fine with staying in. We ordered a pizza, changed into lounge clothes and made ourselves cozy on the sofa after we ate. I convinced him to tell me more of the story he told me on the plane. I laid across the sofa wrapped up in a flannel blanket, with a bunch of throw pillows behind me. Adler was sitting in the middle with my legs across his lap. I closed my eyes so that I could picture in my mind what he was saying. I could feel the emotions of his characters as they came to life. I am so relaxed and feel right at home. I could get used to listening to him talk. His voice is calming and if I'm going to tell the truth, it turns me on. Even if I didn't know what Adler looked like, I'd still want more. Some men can talk and talk and you feel your insides melting just by the sound their voice makes. So much for Adler being an asshole. He's so laid back and nice. I knew back at his office he wasn't going to be a jerk. What boss makes their employees that comfortable at work? He makes them feel like they are working from home. Adler needs to show me another side of him, or I'm in trouble. It's going to be difficult to keep my feelings at bay.

Adler stops talking. I open my eyes and look at him. *"You stop at the worst moments."*

"I stop when I have your attention."

"You've had my attention the whole time."

"I know. Imagine I dangled your favorite treat out in front of you and now you want a bite. I have you on the hook and now you aren't going anywhere. You

could try and leave, but something inside of you needs to know if you'll ever get a bite. That's how you keep readers. If the story goes flat, you lose them and they may not come back."

"Is this one of your books?"

"No, I've made it up as I went along."

"Maybe you should jot it down."

"If I went and wrote what I told you, it wouldn't come out the same. I have to be typing as I tell it or it comes out differently."

"You are an interesting creature, Mr. Vaughn. I can get an image in my mind of a design I want to make, a day or even a week later I can do it to match what I was picturing."

"Emotions play a big part in writing. If you're in the wrong frame of mind it just doesn't work. Whatever you are feeling at the time of writing, it will reflect in the outcome."

A yawn spilled out and I wasn't going to deny I was tired. Adler being the gentleman he is, said he was ready to turn in himself. We went to his bedroom and I crawled right into bed. I was surprised when he tucked me in, kissed my forehead, and told me goodnight. His home is a one bedroom, I expected him to be next to me. Instead I watched him turn out the light on his way out. I felt bad that he is sleeping elsewhere. This is his home, I should be the one to sleep on the sofa. Or better yet, we are adults. We could have shared his bed without having sex. I'll have to bring that up to him tomorrow. Right now, my eyes are heavy and I am too comfy to move.

CHAPTER FIVE
ADLER

I am generally a night owl. So when I put Ciara to bed, I went back out to the living room. I laid on the sofa willing myself to sleep. When that didn't work, I got up and went to my home office. I opened a new word document and recaptured the story I told Ciara. I shocked myself when my fingers and my mind worked together to get every word I spoke to her typed out. I didn't go any further into the story because the rest hasn't been told yet. Who knows if there will be an ending.

Ciara doesn't know that my intention on dating her was to write her love story. Now that I have met her, I don't know if it's possible. I don't think I am capable of listening to her telling me about the other nine men she's been dating. It's one thing to hear about past relationships to learn about the person you are with, but this is entirely different. She hasn't officially broken off any relationship with the other guys. It's more like they are on hold. I'm the last guy in line. I could be the one she picks. I think knowing about her other relationships could tarnish what I want to build with her. If I get her to open up about her feelings, I could very well eliminate myself from the equation. That is something I am not ready to do at this moment. So my condition with Millie is now off the table. I am going to give this relationship my best shot. I am ecstatic to try to be the guy for Ciara. There has been nothing but good vibes since I laid my eyes on her. I look at this as I might have found the woman for me by complete accident.

By the time I made it back to the sofa, I was pretty worn out. Sleep finally came easily. I slept great for the amount of hours of shuteye I got. I am by no means an early riser. If it weren't for the chill in the house, I'd still be in dream land. Instead I am awake at seven. I could have tried using another blanket, but I got up and got the fire going again. In normal circumstances I'd be in my bed with an electric blanket in case it got chilly. This old house doesn't generally get cold once it heats up. The stones help keep it warm if the fire does burn out in the night.

Now that I have the fire going again, I need to find something to occupy my time. I am tempted to make a lot of noise to wake Ciara up. Knowing she is just down the hall, is like being a kid staring at your gifts under the tree. You're all jittery inside with excitement, wanting to know what is hidden inside the box? I am so eager to spend time with Ciara, but I'll be patient and wait for her to wake.

❧

I have a feeling it is going to be a long cold winter. It's only the beginning of October. The high temperature for today is only in the upper forties. I made myself useful and came outside to chop some wood. I'm not sure what this coming winter will bring, but I want to be prepared in case I spend the majority of my time here. I tend to bounce back and forth between here and New York. I am hoping to spend most of my time here. The city is a nice place to live part of the year, however, nothing beats being home. This is where I have roots and also where I do my best writing. It would be nice if Ciara and I stayed put this month. I don't see why we can't unless there is trouble at the office.

CHAPTER 5

I am heading back inside the house when I catch Ciara watching me from the sunroom. I got so excited about seeing her awake, I almost dropped the armful of wood. I would have laughed it off because that's probably what she would do, a small part of me would feel foolish, though. I managed to recover and not drop a single piece. It was great that she opened the door for me.

"Good morning, lumberjack."

I chuckle. *"Good morning, beautiful."* I stack the wood by the fireplace. *"I'd offer you coffee or hot cocoa, but I don't have any."*

"Oh, do you have tea?"

"I don't. How about you get changed and we go into town. There's a nice breakfast joint there and then we can go shopping for supplies."

"Sounds like a plan. Should only take me a few minutes to get ready as long as you are okay with a ponytail in my hair."

Hell she wouldn't even need to comb it and I'd be okay with the way she looks. *"It's quite cool out, so you might want to dress for it."*

"I am so happy I didn't pack cut-offs, I'd freeze my buns off."

I raise my brows. She has no idea what image is

going through my mind right now. Her buns being cold wouldn't happen.

"I noticed you packed light. Before we get supplies, we better get you more clothes."

"Ugh, I'm so sick of shopping for clothes. Grams' rule is ridiculous."

I chuckle to myself as I watch her go down the hallway. Damn her ass is nice in flannel pajama pants. We might need to get her thicker night shirts, or my manhood is going to be hard the entire time she is here. Christ, she is testing my patience and she doesn't even know it. I'm used to one-night stands.

※

We had breakfast in town and it was delightful. It was interesting seeing Ciara and I enjoy the same meal. We both aren't huge on a big breakfast, but this morning cinnamon French toast and bacon hit the spot. She told me she is used to having a muffin or bagel. I am used to drinking a protein shake. I was pleasantly surprised to learn she likes tea over coffee. Most girls are into those fancy lattes or iced coffee that is so strong it could put hair on your chest. I am slowly learning about her likes and dislikes. So far, I am enjoying what I do know.

She isn't what I would consider high maintenance. She is more like the simple women I write about in my books. Don't get me wrong, a simple woman cares about herself and her appearance. She just isn't over the top. She can go out in public without a shower, put her hair up in a ponytail and still feel comfortable in her own skin. Ciara is definitely my type of woman. She proved me more right by her shopping for clothes. I have gone shopping with old girlfriends and Christ it was an all-day event. They had to shop every rack in the store. Ciara, on the other hand, only looked at what caught her eye as she wandered around the store. Who knows maybe her being a clothing designer has made her that way. But from her comment earlier, I'd say she isn't big on getting spoiled.

When Ciara went into the dressing room to try on a dress, I browsed the jewelry section. If she decides to get the dress, I found something I believe would go well with it. I purchase the pieces before she comes out. I saw her add the dress to the buy pile. I cannot wait until she wears it. I am not a fashion kind of guy, but I think I did okay. I'll wait until I get her approval before I go pat myself on the back.

Just as we were leaving the store, a friend of my mother's, Lynn Stiffles was coming in. I introduced the ladies as Lynn was curious who Ciara was. Lynn and my mother were more than friends, they considered each other like sisters. The thing that caught my attention was Lynn mentioning it was the fall festival in town this weekend. I go to it every year if I'm home. If Ciara wants to go, I'd love to take her.

CHAPTER SIX
CIARA

Today was a really nice day with Adler. The town he grew up in is small, but it has amazing clothing stores. I can't forget breakfast this morning, it was so good. It is difficult to find French toast made with actual cinnamon bread. It's even more difficult to find a place that makes it right. Overloaded egg on French toast is a no go. Who wants soggy bread anyway? Not me, so it was perfect. In the back of my mind, I would love to go again before I leave.

Shopping with Adler was kind of fun. He stood back and let me do my thing. He gave his opinion when I asked and wasn't afraid to tell me if something didn't look right. I like honesty and I know telling someone you just met the truth isn't easy because you don't want to hurt their feelings. Usually

I have Porter for that. Adler was a wonderful substitute, though.

I've been putting my new wardrobe away, while Adler said he needed to reply to an email he received while we were grocery shopping. He said it was important or he wouldn't bother with it. I'm fine if he needs to attend to business. Life doesn't stop just because I'm here. Besides, it's more realistic to see how our relationship would go if we were working. It's more difficult for me because I am not working. I don't even know how my career is going to fit into my life in the future. Whoever I end up being with, it's going to be an adjustment for both of us. That is one of the things that weighs heavy on my mind about rushing into a marriage. How are we supposed to know we can balance work and a relationship when we've had no work in the time we were together?

"I've been watching you holding the same pair of jeans in your hand for the last five minutes. What's eating at your mind?"

"Nothing really. Did you reply to your email?"

"I did."

I put the pair of jeans on the shelf in the closet. Adler has a closet full of clothes. His house is full of things, except for food.

"How much time do you spend here?"

"As much as possible, but I'd say probably less than six months a year if I were to put the time all together."

"Does someone look after the place while you are gone?"

"Yes, my friend Judy does."

"Will I be meeting her?"

"She is supposed to stop by sometime this week."

I fold more clothes and put them away. *"Can I ask you something more serious?"*

"You don't need to ask permission to ask me a question."

"Where do you plan on living, if say, we get married?"

"That would be something we'd have to figure out as a couple. We both have a business in New York to consider."

"Do you want children?"

"If the woman I love wants a family, I'm not going to deny her from having my children. But if she doesn't want them, I can live with that, as well."

"That's a great answer, but it doesn't really answer my question. I'm asking what you want, not what the woman wants."

"Would I like a son or daughter or possibly both? I'd like to think I would someday. If that day ever

comes, I want to make sure my relationship with my wife is strong enough to withstand any storm. I don't want to have a family with someone then end up divorced. I was raised that way, and it wasn't a picnic."

"I'm sorry that happened to you."

"Do you want kids?"

"Honestly, I don't really know yet."

I put the last of my clothes away. Now that the question has been turned on me, I'd like a change of subject. I'm glad when he does change it.

"I was wondering if you'd be my date to the fall festival tomorrow night."

"I'd love to be your date."

"Perfect! We can get food while we are there! You are going to love it."

"Speaking of food. I'm starving."

"Do you want to go out or stay in and cook?"

"Actually, I would like to make you dinner, if that's okay."

"I would like that a lot. Home cooked meals are rare to come by for me."

We go to the kitchen and I start taking things out of the refrigerator and put it all on the counter. I find the dry ingredients I need and look everything over to make sure I have everything. Adler asks if he can help with anything, I tell him no thank you because I want to try this on my own. I proceeded to tell him how I am really not at all into cooking meals from scratch, but that I recently learned how to make this meal. I didn't bother telling him Wyatt taught me. I'm sure he can figure out on his own that one of the guys taught me.

"I really feel like I should be doing something."

"I have an idea. How about you start reading one of your books to me?"

"I sound like an idiot when I read out loud. I'm not even joking when I say that."

With his voice that is smooth as butter, I doubt that's true. *"You know you left me hanging again last night. I need to know if the coffee girl showed up or if Alex overslept and missed her entirely."*

"That is something I can do."

I see him sitting across the counter from me, through my lashes. He taps an icon on his phone. I smile. I bet he's going to write this story.

Adler is a kind soul. So far I don't know if we are compatible for a long term relationship or not. Lincoln and my relationship started slow, but there were feelings for one another by the end of our time together. Whatever way my relationship turns out with Adler, I think he's someone I want in my life.

Only time will tell if we are meant to be friends and lovers or just friends.

※

We had dinner and I was so happy I did so well with Wyatt's recipe. Adler kept complimenting me on how good it was. I think I was blushing by the time we were done eating. I have never been complimented on my cooking before.

After our dinner settled, we changed into comfy clothes and Adler suggested we have a fire outside. I made us hot cocoa with peppermint cream while he started a fire for us. I grabbed us a couple of blankets on the way outdoors. It was nice to relax and have absolutely no stress. I listened to Adler telling me a story about the times his dad would take him camping as a kid. The way he talks about his father, I wonder what made him say growing up with divorced parents wasn't a picnic. I wanted to ask, but I'm hoping he tells me in his own time. I don't keep it a secret that I didn't have a father. That's pretty much as far as I talk about that.

When it was late and we were ready to call it a night, we came inside. Adler did the same as he did the night before. He tucked me in bed and was going to sleep on the sofa. I told him he needed to sleep in his bed. I'd go to the sofa if he wanted me to. He was very hesitant in getting in beside me. I told him I'd be a good girl and stay on my side. When the lights turned out, I reached over and held his hand. That's how I fell asleep.

CHAPTER SEVEN
ADLER

Ciara suggested I get ready for the fall festival before her. I only have one bathroom, so I was okay with it. I came out dressed in faded black jeans, a light gray button-down, and a black suit jacket. If I were going to the festival alone, I'd wear a sweater or something like that. I am taking Ciara on a date, so I want to look nice for her. I probably should have trimmed up my face, but I tend to keep the five o'clock shadow. It's a little longer than I keep it, but I think it looks alright.

"Mr. Vaughn, you are looking like you are going out on a date. Who's the lucky lady?"

I really like the sound of her laughter. *"Just some woman I met."*

"Do I know her?"

"You probably do. She's from New York."

"That's a shame you already have a date. I was hoping you'd take me out tonight."

"For you, I will cancel any date to have you on my arm."

She puts a hand over her heart. *"Awe, aren't you just the sweetest."* She gets off the sofa and comes across the room to where I am. *"When you cancel your date, let her down easy."* She kisses my cheek and my heart starts thumping in my chest. *"I'm going to get ready for our date."*

"I am going to be the luckiest man there tonight with you beside me."

Her hand comes to my face. *"Nah, Adler, I'm the lucky one."*

I watch her over my shoulder as she heads down the hall toward my bedroom. Once she crosses the hall to go into the bathroom, I go to my office. I sit at my desk and open the word document to type out the part of the story I told her while she made dinner last night.

Instead of my fingers moving along the keys, I find myself getting lost in thoughts of last night. Sleeping next to Ciara and not touching her in the ways I want to touch her was very challenging. I had to lay there in the dark willing myself to be good. She made it even more difficult when she reached over and held my hand. I cannot say that I ever just held hands with a woman before while trying to sleep. Although I wanted to do more with her, it was satisfying to just hold her hand.

I try to think of a time that I have felt this smitten with a lady before. I have had girlfriends in the past, but feelings never came close to what I am already feeling for Ciara. I believe I have found the kind of woman I have in all my books. That sort of scares me, but in a good way. It's nice to know that this kind of woman really does exist in the real world.

꙳

When getting lost in thought, you don't really realize how time can pass. I hadn't realized that is what happened to me until I looked up and saw Ciara in the doorway. My god this woman makes my heart thump in my chest. Every time I think I saw her beauty, she proves me wrong. Ciara is a gorgeous piece of art that you can't take your eyes off of. I knew back at the store that the dress she was trying on would look perfect on her. Now that I am feasting my eyes on her, it's better than I could have imagined.

"Am I overdressed?"

CHAPTER 7

"Absolutely not. You are missing something, though."

She raises her brows. *"I don't know what I could possibly be missing."*

I get up from my desk and go to her, taking her small hand in mine. *"Come with me."*

Ciara follows me to the bedroom, then we go into the walk-in closet. I open a small wooden box and take out the jewelry I bought the other day for her. She opens the velvet box and she looks at me.

"It's beautiful."

"Not as beautiful as you are."

She takes the necklace out and holds it out to me. *"Can you help me put it on?"*

"I'd love to."

I take her to the full length mirror and stand behind her. She lifts her hair out of the way. I latch the necklace at the back of her neck. I watch in the mirror as her hair falls all around her back and shoulders. I was right. The black onyx necklace goes perfect with the gray sweater dress. The black leather, knee-high boots and black belt helps the black onyx of the jewel stand out even more.

Her hand touches the necklace. *"Thank you, Adler, I love it."*

"There's another box you haven't opened yet."

I reach over and hand the other box to her. She opens the box and takes out the matching tennis bracelet. *"I have never been given something like this before."*

"You deserve to be spoiled, Ciara."

"I don't know. This must have cost you a lot of money."

I take the onyx tennis bracelet out of the velvet box and put it on her wrist. *"It's worth every cent to see the smile it put on your beautiful face."*

Ciara gets up on her tiptoes and kisses my cheek, then faces the mirror once more. I see her hands trembling as she touches the necklace again. I believe her that a man hasn't done anything like this for her before. It's a shame men don't shower her with gifts. They must be complete fools or idiots. I know the men she's been dating in the last nine months have money, if they didn't buy her jewelry, what did they give her? What if I'm doing something wrong? My heart thumps in my chest just thinking about the possibility she thinks I am trying to buy her love. Fuck, I hope I didn't mess this up.

"I was right earlier when I said I was the lucky one."

I snap out of my thoughts and look at her reflection in the mirror. Her smile tells me I didn't fuck up. My shoulders relax as relief washes over me.

"Ms. Verbank, are you ready for a night on the town with me?"

"I am ready, Mr. Vaughn."

❦

When we arrive in town, we begin walking toward the festival holding hands. The sound of fallen leaves crunch beneath our feet. The smell of fall stirs as we walk. The smell of food cooking lingers in the air the closer we get to the festival, overtaking the fall scent entirely. The festival has brought many townspeople out. It always does. Bringing Ciara here means a lot to me. I can't help but feel like a young man on his first date ever. I want to impress the girl. I want her to want to come back to Kentucky with me. If this works out between us, this fall festival could be the first. We could make this trip every year. A tradition to celebrate our first date.

"Are you hungry?"

"I could wait a while."

We had a late lunch today. I figured she would want to wait a while, but I wanted to make sure.

We start browsing the craft tents. A few times Ciara smelled candles and put a couple to my nose. She laughed when I made a face at the pumpkin spice one. I did end up buying the cinnamon apple one for her. We stopped off at another tent and bought matching sweatshirts with the festival logo on it. I also bought her a hand crafted wooden box to keep her jewelry in.

After we went through all the craft tents, we ended up in the section where they have rides and games. We played a few. Ciara wasn't as lucky at them as I was. I won her a few teddy bears by throwing a baseball at bottles. I think my new favorite thing to do is putting a smile on her face.

Just as we were ready to decide what we wanted to eat, I saw a photo booth. I dragged her in with me. She tried to protest, but I wasn't having it. My favorite picture is of her sitting on my lap with our tongues stuck out at each other. Our laughter died when I kissed her for the first time. I thought my heart thumped in my chest before, but holy hell, I was wrong. Kissing this woman is indescribable. I could never leave this photo booth ever again and be satisfied. Ciara is the woman I want to date for a very long time. I don't believe a month is going to be long enough.

CHAPTER EIGHT
CIARA

We stayed at the festival for the midnight fireworks. They were definitely worth staying for. My date with Adler was one of the best dates I've ever had. Our date was out of the normal for me and I won't ever forget this night. At first, it reminded me of the night Hawk took me to the pier. This was different, though. Hawk and I had to run off to hide from the media after a Ferris wheel ride and shopping in a store. Adler and I got to enjoy the entire night without any hassles. It really was incredible.

I am in the bathroom, ready to change into night clothes. I find myself touching the necklace he gave me. Knowing Adler took the time to pick it, melts my heart. Him giving me this really means a lot to me. It's one of the sweetest gestures anyone has done for me. Every minute I spend with him, my guard is slipping. I didn't want to like him, but I already do. He makes it easy to like him. Why couldn't he be a jerk? Why does he have to add to my already difficult choice? Grams must have a magical way of finding the world's greatest bachelors and got all nine of them to put a bid in to date me. I don't know what magical wand she waved, but I wish I could borrow it so that I pick the right husband.

"Need help getting that off?"

"Yes, please."

He puts the wooden box he bought me on the vanity. I moved my hair out of the way and he unlatched the necklace. He then lifts my hands, palm up and puts the necklace in it. I reach over and put it in the box. Adler turns me to face him. I stare at his face as he takes the bracelet off my wrist. Adler is a very attractive man. That kiss earlier was passionate. He hasn't kissed me since the photo booth, but I'm hoping he does again soon. Soon, as in right now would be nice.

"Ciara."

"Adler."

"I want to kiss you."

"I want yo…"

The feel of his hand placed softly on my face

stops my words from finishing. I close my eyes as his head bends to kiss me. He kisses my forehead, my nose, then my lips. I put my hands around his neck as I got up on my tiptoes. His arms wrap around my waist, bringing his body closer to mine. We kiss until the air in our lungs is gone. He stares into my eyes as I comb my fingers through his five o'clock shadow. When I think he'll kiss me again, he proves me wrong by speaking instead.

"I sliced the grape pie I bought for us."

I smile. *"I can't wait to taste it. I'm just going to get out of this dress and into something more comfortable,"* I say while I slide my hands into his suit jacket and remove it entirely. I see him inhale.

"What are you doing?"

I reach for the first button that isn't already undone. *"Helping you get more comfortable."*

Before I can finish unbuttoning his shirt, I pull it from the waistband of his jeans. Then undo the last few buttons. I open the front of his shirt and place my hands on his chest. I lean in and get up on my tiptoes to kiss the crook of his neck. I put my hands on the button of his jeans. I don't think twice about opening the front.

I whisper in his ear. *"Are you more comfortable?"*

He clears his throat to say something when I take a few steps away from him. I undo the belt around my waist and drop it. I bend and grab the hem of my sweater dress and slowly wiggle my way out of it. I put a hand to the vanity and unzip my knee high boots to remove them. I don't look at him until I am left with nothing on but a matching bra and panties. His eyes travel over my almost naked body. I spin around so that my back is to him. I look at him in the mirror. Then I turn my head and see him over my shoulder.

"I think I need your help."

Adler puts his hand on my stomach and yanks my body back to his. He moves my hair off to one side and kisses my shoulder, then the side of my neck.

"If I didn't know any better, I'd say you are a naughty girl, Ms. Verbank. I'm all for sex on the first date, are you?"

"If you'd rather just eat pie, we can do that instead."

His hand slides into my panties and I arch my back, letting my ass press against his front. I moan when his fingers enter me. I whine when those very fingers that felt so good left my body. My lips part slightly. I gasp at the feel of his finger outlining my lips. Holy shit my heart is pounding in my chest. Adler spins me around to face him. His mouth is on me quicker than I can catch my breath. He moans as our lips part and his tongue slips into my mouth. Jesus, I need air. I catch my breath when he lifts me off my feet and I wrap my legs around his waist. He carries me to his bedroom, then sits on the edge of his bed. He moves my hair out of the way and kisses to the top of my breasts. I feel him undoing my bra. His fingers graze my skin as he slides the straps off my shoulders.

"Put your knee on the bed."

I straddle his lap while on my knees. My chest is right there in his face. He fills his hands and sucks a nipple into his mouth. One hand moves between my legs where he pushes my panties off to the side. His fingers enter me again. My body reacts to everything he's doing to me. I want more. I want to feel his cock inside me. I try to push my panties past my hips, but Adler rips them off me instead. He then manages to get his jeans off. He groans as I lower myself down onto him. My nails dig into his flesh as I take in all of him. I move my hips back and forth. He feels amazing inside of me.

Three positions and two orgasms later. Adler and I get into bed. I snuggle up next to him and he kisses the top of my head.

"You better not ghost me tomorrow."

I laugh. *"Oh, hell no. I still haven't tried that grape pie you rave about."*

"Good night, Ciara."

"Good night, Alder."

CHAPTER NINE
ADLER

The first week being with Ciara has flown by so fast. Literally time can slow down. I have three weeks left to win this woman's heart. Three weeks left to give her mine. Can it be done? I'm not positive it can be. I'm also not against the idea that it can be done. Life has a funny way of working and I'm sure going to give it my best shot. On paper Ciara is the perfect woman for me. The reality is my life right now isn't a romance novel and I can't flip to the last chapter to see if it's a happy ending. I can only embrace these next three weeks with Ciara and make every minute count for something.

Today will start with Ciara getting to meet my dear friend, Judy. Tonight, I made reservations at a restaurant for us to enjoy an evening out. The last few nights have consisted of staying in and enjoying one another's company. I told Ciara more of the story I am making up as I tell it. She seems to like my storytelling. It's flowed out of me so easily, even I am liking where it's going.

Ciara comes into the living room with a huge smile on her face. She's been in my office doing something that I wasn't allowed to see. My curiosity is at an all-time high. I am hoping to see that she is making good use of the journal I gave her yesterday.

"I have been on the phone with my friend Porter. He just told me that I have been chosen by Cora Winterstorm to design the clothing for her and Asher's upcoming movie."

"That's fantastic news."

"This is really big for me and for the MV clothing line."

I have no idea who she is speaking about. Ciara comes to sit next to me on the sofa. I can read her expression, she has more news to share. She seems a little hesitant to share. She must be able to read mine as well.

"You don't know who Cora is, do you?"

"I do know who she is." She raises an eyebrow. I laugh. *"Okay, you got me, I don't know."*

"The actress from the movie Grumpy Santa."

"Oh, the chick who landed Asher Magnus."

"Oh my God, Adler, you did not just say that. He landed her, by the way."

"Really, that's exciting news for you. I'm happy for you." Ciara nervously bites her nails. *"What's the matter, Ciara?"*

"In order for me to do this, I have to go back to New York."

"Okay, when?"

"Tomorrow."

"Okay, so I'll have the jet fueled and ready to go."

"Really?"

"Yes, really! Your career is important to you. I'm not going to hold you back from it."

Ciara leaps her body onto mine. She kisses me, then her expression turns all serious. *"You are coming with me, right?"*

"I think I am going to stay here and finish writing that story. You are welcome to come back when you finish up in New York."

Her eyes go wide. *"We would lose a week together."*

"Absence makes the heart grow fonder they say."

"Adler, you have to come with me. Please!"

"Is that begging I hear in your voice?"

"If that's what it sounds like, then yes."

"I kinda like it when you beg, Ms. Verbank."

"So, you'll come with me?"

I sit up straighter on the sofa, fill my hands with her ass, and kiss her. *"I might need some more convincing."*

"Oh you play dirty, Mr. Vaughn."

I'm just about to get more flirty with the hot chick sitting on my lap, when the front door opens. Horrible timing, Judy! I whisper, *"Of course I'm coming with you to New York. I'm not willing to give up any of my time with you."*

"Oh, I see how you play, Adler." She winks at me before getting off my lap.

Judy makes her way into the living room. She takes one look at me, then Ciara, back to me. I know that smile. She knows she probably interrupted us about to rip our clothes off.

I got off the sofa to give Judy a hug. *"Judy, meet Ciara Verbank. Ciara, this is Judy Halloran, my friend and my editor."*

"It's a pleasure to meet you, Ciara."

"Likewise. So, you get to read Adler's words before anyone else?"

"I do. I'm lucky he trusts me with his work."

"Ladies, shall I get us some drinks?"

"I wish I could stay for one, but I'm kind of in a

hurry. Elizabeth is eager for me to edit so that she can get her hands on the next book."

"Elizabeth that I met at your office?"

"Yes, she is my second editor."

"That's nice." Ciara gets off the sofa to stand next me. *"Judy, please stay. I'd love to get to know you better. I'm sure you can tell me some secrets about this big guy right here."*

"I'll get us some drinks. You ladies can gossip while I'm gone."

Judy rubs her hands together like she's got juicy gossip to spill about me. They sit on the sofa facing each other. I'm not worried. I have amazing friends in my circle. I trust all my girls fully.

Today was simply amazing. Seeing my friend getting along so well with my girlfriend is a relief. There have been a few short relationships I've had over the years that none of my girls cared for who I was seeing. I say seeing because I haven't had a true girlfriend in years. If Ciara is going to be in my life, it's important to me that my friends like her. It just makes life that much more enjoyable.

I've been on the phone with my pilot for the last

half an hour getting everything ready for tomorrow. I'm looking forward to seeing Ciara in her element. Clearly her career means a great deal to her. I'll take this opportunity to learn more about her and her work. I'm elated I get this chance to see how work life will blend with our relationship life.

Now that I'm off the phone, I check my watch. Our dinner reservations are within the hour. I better check to see how close Ciara is to being ready.

When I enter the bedroom, Ciara is sitting on the bed with her back to the doorway. I knock on the wooden frame so that she knows I'm here. She looks at me over her shoulder and holds up her finger to say give me a minute. Should I leave her to her privacy? If I stay I don't want her to think I'm eavesdropping. Damn, I am out of practice how this works. I should leave. Let her have her privacy.

Just when I'm about to turn and leave, I hear her say goodbye to whomever she's talking to.

"Sorry about that. I had to tell Grams about Cora."

"It's no problem."

"I just need to get my shoes on then I'm ready for our date."

Ciara is dressed in a pair of tight black jeans and a red loose fitting sweater. The collar is so wide cut, it falls off one shoulder. She isn't wearing any jewelry. I wish I bought her more than the pieces I did buy for her the other day. She should be showered in jewelry. I could suggest she wears the necklace, but I don't want to make her feel she needs to wear it.

"I hope you like escargot. DiGotti serves the best I have ever had."

"Sorry, but I won't be putting that in my mouth."

I laugh so hard, I almost fall over. *"What will you put in your mouth?"*

"If you are good, you might find out."

"Good, huh? Not sure I know what you mean."

"I guess you'll be in suspense until later."

"I think you are a tease."

"I think we better get this date started."

"I couldn't agree more!"

I spanked her ass as she passed by me. I laugh when she yelped and rubbed her butt where my hand landed.

CHAPTER TEN
CIARA

Adler has brought me to a very nice place for dinner. The lighting is low, and candles are lit on every table. There is soft music playing in the background. Most tables consist of couples, enjoying one another's company. You can feel the romance in the air. We are taken to a balcony where we are seated. Our table overlooks the rest of the diners. I take a look at the menu and the prices are decent for how elegant this place is. When I look at the appetizers, I laugh to myself. Flipping the page to the entrees, I see right away what I'm ordering, so I close the menu and place it on the table. Adler puts his menu down on top of mine.

"Escargot, huh?"

"Ya, I was kidding about that. I wouldn't want you to put that in your mouth, anyway."

Why does he have to have such a charming smile?

Literally he's too damn sexy when he smiles. He makes my girly parts tingle.

"Oh, I know exactly what I'm putting in my mouth."

"Hmm, I can't wait to see what that is."

"What is making your mouth water?"

"Baby, I don't think you want me to answer that question."

"I think I do want you to answer."

"It's top secret, so if you want to know, you have to come closer."

We are interrupted by the waitress that is ready to take our order. He smiles at me and winks. I wish he'd stop doing that. He's turning my insides to mush. I turn my attention to the lovely young lady, I feel it's written all over my blushing cheeks what Adler is doing to me. We placed our order, I am surprised that he ordered exactly what I did. I guess I won't be trading meals with him if I don't like mine.

"So, Buffalo chicken lasagna is making your mouth water, huh?"

"Nah, that's just to fill my belly. I told ya it's a secret."

I scoot my body closer to him. I put my hand on his thigh. *"I'm listening."*

"I can trust you with my secrets?"

"Most definitely."

"If I tell you, you can't laugh."

I laugh. *"I cross my heart I won't laugh."*

Adler puts his mouth near my ear. *"What makes my mouth water is lemon drops."*

I burst out laughing. I was not expecting him to say that. *"I'm sorry,"* I try to say with a straight face.

"What really makes my mouth water is thinking about laying you on my bed, spreading your legs, and filling my tastebuds with your sweet pussy."

"Mmm."

"It's too bad I can't clear this table, lay you out on top of it, and have a taste right this second."

"Ya, that's definitely too bad. I wish I could help you out."

Jesus, he is making my panties wet. Would he be offended if I suggested we get our dinner to go? I am all for helping him fill his hunger.

"Reach into my pocket and take what I have inside it to the bathroom with you."

"Huh?"

He raises his brow at me. I'm almost scared to see what it is. However curiously I need to know what he has. I reach in his suit jacket outer pocket and grab what's inside it. My eyes go wide.

CHAPTER 10

"Put it in your purse, go to the bathroom and put it in place."

I swallow. His eyes tell me he's not joking. I open my purse and drop the sex toy inside. I hope I don't regret this. This is out of my comfort zone.

I get up from the table and head down the stairs to find the restroom. As I pass tables, I swear everyone knows what I'm about to do. I can feel my cheeks burning up. When I reach the bathroom, I go to the sink and turn the water on. I look in the mirror, my face looks normal. I sigh with relief. I turn the water off without splashing my face with cool water. I tell myself I can do this. I go into a stall and pull my pants down, then open my purse. I study the toy before inserting it inside me. I hurry and pull up my pants so that I don't change my mind. I wash my hands and leave the bathroom.

"I thought I saw you come in with the new guy."

I know that voice. I turn around to see who is behind me. I want to run.

"What are you doing here, Hunter?"

"I'm out to dinner with a colleague. As I said, I thought I saw you come in."

"So you followed me to the bathroom?"

"Actually, I didn't. I was just leaving the restroom myself."

"I gotta go," I say walking away.

"Ciara, wait," he says, *"please."*

"What do you want?"

"I've been trying to call you since I saw you at that concert in July."

"I don't know what you are talking about. I do not have any missed calls from you. Why are you calling me anyway?"

"I have been calling, but I have a new number."

"Just tell me what you want. I have a date waiting for me."

"It's about that guy who punched me in the face. You know the first one you dated after me."

I am trying to keep my cool here. *"What about Malcolm?"*

"I didn't set his place on fire."

"Guilty conscience? I never accused you of doing that."

"I know who did."

I almost want to laugh. *"Enlighten me."*

"I believe your mother did. She found me back in June and asked me if I wanted to get back at you and Millie. She told me her plan and as much as I wanted to get even with Malcolm for punching me, I wasn't about to become a criminal doing it."

CHAPTER 10

"Thanks for the information. I really have to go."

"Ciara, I came to your opening to tell you, but that didn't go as planned. I hope you find what you are looking for. I know I'm not it."

My mouth feels like it's on the floor as he walks away. I don't know if I should believe him or not. Oddly, I sort of do. I suck in a breath as I fall into the wall. The toy inside me has been turned on. The vibration inside me makes me remember I have Adler waiting at our table. I wait until the vibration stops before I take a step out of this hallway. Once I recover and get my bearings, I make my way through the maze of tables with my head angled down. I don't think I can bear to look at anyone. I just about run up the stairs when I reach them. I slide into the big booth and get another reminder of what's inside me. I take one look at Adler.

"I can't believe you did that to me."

"So you didn't leave it in your purse?" He leans over to my ear. *"That makes me hard knowing that I have control over your body right now."*

The waitress comes with our food. I squeeze my thighs together as she places the plates on the table. I glance at the food on my plate.

"Is there anything else I can get you?"

I speak up. *"Yes, I'm feeling a little out of sorts. Do you mind having our dinners wrapped up to go, please."*

She is surprised at my request and looks at Adler. He nods his head for confirmation. If I didn't have a sex toy in my pussy vibrating right this second, I'd be irritated. I hold my breath, terrified I'm going to slip and let out a moan. I just want to get the hell out of here.

The toy turns off. I let out a deep breath. Adler gives his credit card for the waitress to settle the bill. Good because the sooner we can leave, the happier I'll be.

"You play dirty, Mr. Vaughn."

He just smiles, then says, *"My mouth is watering."*

This evening is nothing like how I expected it to go. I thought this was going to be a nice, relaxing dinner out. Instead, I run into Hunter while I have a sex toy inside me from my new boyfriend. The toy is at least enjoyable. Seeing Hunter not so much. I would love to forget I saw Hunter, but that is difficult knowing he's in the same place as me.

Adler signs the bill and then puts his credit card away. *"Ready?"*

"Definitely."

Adler opens the car door for me. I get in and buckle up. He puts our dinner in the backseat before getting in himself. He starts the car. Instead of driving away he twists in his seat to face me.

"Are you alright?"

"I'm sorry I wanted to leave. I saw someone I used to know and I just wanted to get away from him."

"Don't apologize for that. I'm not upset about leaving at all. My main concern is you and your well-being."

"I'm better now."

"Good."

I feel even better when Adler pulls out onto the road. I watch out the window at the side mirror, paying close attention to the headlights behind us. I see a few cars turn off before we do. I relax the further we get away. I don't think Hunter is following us. Once we drive out of the small city and we are the only ones on the road, I feel even better. I feel my anxiety washing away.

I grip the door and the edge of the seat when the toy comes to life. My thighs clench together as the vibration inside me gets faster. A moan slips out past my lips. The higher the speed, the more I press my lower body into the seat as my back arches. Holy hell! I am on the verge of an orgasm.

Suddenly the car comes to a stop. And so does the toy. My chest is pumping hard. I can't ask what he's doing in the middle of nowhere because my body is in a heaping mess of sexual arousal. Adler gets out of the car and comes to my side, opening the door. He wants me to get out? I don't think I'm able to walk anywhere, let alone stand on my own. Adler swoops me into his arms, taking me out of the car. He sets me on the hood. I look around at nothing when he begins taking my pants off. The toy that's still inside me comes back to life. He scoots my body closer to the edge of the hood then starts fucking me with the toy. I can barely hold myself upright. I lie back on the warm hood when he sucks my clit into his mouth. I'm a goner and cum moments later. Once the toy is removed, he replaces it with his tongue, until the orgasm passes. I am trying to regain my composure so that I can return the favor. I watch Adler undo his jeans and push them down. He holds his manhood to my pussy. I squirm when he thrusts inside me in one swift move. I try to hold onto the edge of the car as Adler pounds his cock inside me deep. Good fucking gracious, he feels so good.

I didn't have another orgasm before Adler had his

release. The first one was so damn good it didn't even bother me. Adler said he was sorry he couldn't hold back any longer. He said he'll make it up to me when we get home. I'm perfectly satisfied already. He laughs when I say he has to feed me first.

CHAPTER ELEVEN
ADLER

This has been a crazy week. After the first day of going to work with her, I realized I was distracting her from getting the job done. I decided that I might as well do some work myself. I would drop Ciara off at her store and head to my office and at the end of the day, I'd pick her up. Since I wiped my schedule clean for the month, I didn't have much to do. I basically sat around and shot the shit with Elizabeth and the other ladies. A couple days this week, I have taken Ciara lunch at her store and we ate together in her back room. I don't mind at all that she's working, but we are missing valuable time together. We only have so much of it together. By the time evenings roll around, she is still stuck in work mode. It's been challenging to get her attention. I totally get how important this job is to her, so I'm trying to be patient. I'm not an idiot, I know this week would have been different if I actually had work to put my attention on, like her. I don't want to be one of those whiny bitch boyfriends. Today is supposed to be her last day working with Cora. I am hoping that her focus comes back to me. I know that sounds selfish, but it's the truth.

This last hour is dragging. I wish there was something to do to speed up the time. Unfortunately, I have no work on my desk. Elizabeth took the day off and Judy is in Kentucky. I tried calling her about an hour ago and got no answer. It's hard to say this because it's something I never say, but I'm bored out of my goddamn mind.

I pick up my phone. I really don't want to bother Ciara, but what if there's a possibility she can wrap her day up early? If I just send her a quick text message, it's better than sitting here wondering.

Me: Any chance you'll be done early?

Luckily I don't have to wait for a reply.

Ciara: Omg! I wish!

Me: Not the answer I was hoping for.

Ciara: At the rate I'm going, I'm not even sure I'll be done in an hour.

An hour I could handle, but longer is going to drive me insane. I can sit in my office and watch the clock slowly tic by, or I could just go home.

Ciara: I'm sorry, Adler. I didn't think this would take up so much of my time.

Me: Do you think you'll be ready for our dinner date? We have reservations at that restaurant you wanted to take me to.

I wait for her reply. Five minutes… ten minutes. I get no reply.

Me: I'll just cancel.

I gather up my belongings and power off my computer. If I sit here one more minute, I'm going to go crazy. I've been pretty damn patient all week. It's not like me to lose my cool. I feel if I don't find something to do to occupy my time, I'll turn into the whiny bitch boyfriend. That would not be good for our relationship.

 ❧

I went ahead and canceled the dinner reservations. After not hearing back from Ciara. I also left my office and came to my condo in the city. It was driving me just as crazy sitting around here as it did at work. I tried to start a new novel, but my mind wasn't in it. I tried to jump forward in the story I've been telling her and couldn't do that either. I find myself in an odd place. In the past I

CHAPTER 11

wouldn't put my life on hold for a woman. Nothing has ever stopped me in my tracks like this has. I have real feelings for Ciara. I know this because, as I said, I've never put my life on hold for anyone. I'm not used to these sort of feelings I'm developing. I can write about relationships all day. In reality, I'm a little lost. I'm not used to thinking about my own future. I need to figure out if Ciara's head is still in this relationship.

After this week with all her attention on her career. I'm not feeling confident she's still in this with me.

My phone notification sound went off. I reach for my phone.

Ciara: I'm so sorry, I got distracted. I didn't mean to ghost you.

Me: Are you anywhere near being done?

Ciara: I wish. There are some changes with the wardrobe. I'm trying my hardest to finalize everything tonight so that you have my full attention.

Me: Just let me know when I'm picking you up.

Ciara: It could be really late. I can just take a cab.

Think Adler, think! I put my phone down and pace the living space for some time. I know how a working woman works when they get lost in their job. I have come up with a plan to turn this night around.

It will take me less than an hour to put my plan into action.

※

I walk into Ciara's store with confidence that I'm not going to fuck this relationship up. I went ahead and ordered from the restaurant we were supposed to go to tonight for dinner. I took my best guess of what she'd order. In another bag, I took things from my condo to turn her office into a romantic atmosphere so that we could at least enjoy dinner and a little time together as a couple. This evening doesn't need to be a total loss. One thing I know about people when they get caught up in work on a time crunch, they forget to eat.

As soon as the door closes behind me, Porter looks up from whatever he's doing on a computer. He looks at my hands with bags in them and I see worry across his face.

"What are you doing here," he asks.

"Ciara in the back room?"

"She left an hour ago."

"To go where?"

"Cora invited her to dinner with Asher at their place here in the city."

CHAPTER 11

"I see."

"The two of them decided they needed food and to work online. Didn't you get her message? She texted close to forty-five minutes ago."

I am irritated. She blew off our dinner date but is having dinner with Cora and Asher. I went to all this work to make a nice little dinner for two because I thought she'd be here for hours to come. I didn't get a text from Ciara. I set the bags down and take out my phone. For some stupid reason, I want to show Porter I didn't. I look at my screen. Fuck, I do have a missed text. That goddamn button on the side pisses me off. I can't begin to tell you how many times my phone goes on silent without my knowledge. I open it to read it. While I prepared for this mini date, I'm supposed to go to her clients home for dinner. I'm already late.

I look at Porter. Picking up the bag of food I set down, I say, *"Hope you are hungry!"*

"I am! You better boogie, if you don't want to miss dinner."

CHAPTER TWELVE
CIARA

I have felt horrible all week about not spending much time with Adler. I am hopeful that he understands what this meant to me. This was huge for the MV clothing line, and even bigger for me. I was so honored that I got chosen for their wardrobe. It has nothing to do with the celebrity status. I am such a fan of Cora and Asher's love story. That's what it all boiled down to for me.

I know Adler was put on the back burner, so to speak, but this job is only temporary. We still have plenty of time left to spend together. I hope at least. When he didn't show up to dinner, my concerns grew rapidly for our relationship. Maybe he has already given up on our love story. I don't really know because we haven't had time to talk. When I came in late last night, I found him passed out in a chair. I tried to wake him, but it didn't work. I could smell the alcohol on his breath. I left him there and changed my clothing. I went to bed minutes later. I laid in bed for quite some time thinking about Adler. He's such a fantastic guy. He's a romantic at heart, that's a given. Lord knows he's hot as hell. Everything I know so far about him, I like. At this point in our relationship, I'm not sure if he's the one. I would love to find out in the time we do have left together. That is if our relationship hasn't blown up already. This week might have been a true test for him and me. If we fail because I worked, what might my career do to the other relationships I was in? I don't see me giving up everything I worked so hard for, for marriage. I've asked myself from the start, what if I fall in love and give my heart to someone and this whole process fails. I cannot bear the thought of putting my heart on the line for nothing.

My mind was on overload last night and has left me emotionally exhausted. So much so that it's four in the afternoon and I'm just now waking up. If it weren't for Porter calling me, I might still be passed out.

I answered his call to learn everything Cora

wanted has been shipped. I felt a little bit of stress lifting off my shoulders. However that was short lived. I felt a ton of weight settling in after Porter told me to thank Adler for the dinner last night. I didn't have a clue what he meant until I asked. It's no wonder why he didn't show last night at Cora's. I screwed up his romantic dinner he planned. I want to crawl into a hole when Porter tells me all about the candles, nice dinnerware, and flowers Adler had with him. I totally feel like a piece of shit. I was disappointed when he didn't show up, I can't imagine how he must have felt. I need to fix this!

Just as I am about to leap out of bed, my phone goes off again. This time, it's a text from Wyatt.

Wyatt: Sorry it has taken me longer than I wanted to get back to you. I was put on a case that I could not refuse. I checked out the number you gave me. Hunter never went anywhere near Malcolm's home or state for that matter.

Me: Thank you so much for looking into it.

Wyatt: You are welcome. I miss you like fucking crazy!

Me: I miss you, too! I need to go though.

It's true, I do miss Wyatt tremendously. Whenever I think about him, it warms my heart and makes me sad at the same time. I don't ever want to say goodbye to Wyatt, ever!

I ran to the master bathroom to brush my teeth and ran my fingers through my hair before I looked for Adler. His condo is very nice and very large. I prefer his place in Kentucky. It feels more like a real home there. His condo is bare compared to his house. There's nothing really personal here to make this place homey.

"Hey," I say when I find him in his home office.

"Hey."

"I can't believe you let me sleep the entire day."

"You must have needed the rest."

Okay, this isn't the charming Adler I have come to know. This person before me is barely acknowledging that I am in the room. My fears are coming true, my work life does interfere with my relationship life. Maybe that is why I have dated men like Hunter in the past. Men like Hunter don't really care to have my time. I can work my life away without anyone caring.

"Adler, would you look at me."

He looks up from his computer and leans back in his chair. He is looking at me, but it's a very distant look.

"You have my full attention."

I come around to his side of the desk and lean on

it. He swivels in his chair and slides it back, inching away from me.

"First, I want to say I don't know what happened last night. I thought you would have met me for dinner. I was upset that you didn't show up."

"I was going to come. I was halfway there when I turned around and came home instead. We had dinner plans. I guess I was upset, as well."

"I can understand that. I'm sorry plans got changed. It wasn't my intention to upset you. Porter told me about you coming to my store. I feel horrible that I missed what would have been an incredible night with you."

"We have known each other for two weeks. This week has shown me you care very deeply for your career. And that is amazing. The dedication you put into what you love to do is powerful. I don't have a problem with that part of you."

I stand from the desk. I feel my defense coming to light. *"What part of me don't you like?"*

"That didn't come out right. I like everything about you."

"I'm finding that hard to believe. You are very careful with your words, Adler. Please tell me my faults."

*"I'm not perfect, Ciara, even I can mess up my

words. This week has been a hiccup in our relationship. I cleared my schedule to be with you. I have absolutely no problem with you working. I just feel you could have managed your time better. I bent myself over backwards to be with you. I didn't really see you bending that much for me."

"I have a problem with getting caught up in my work when I have a task at hand. I know I have that flaw. I'm not perfect either. When we have had time together this week, you had my full attention."

"I appreciate that."

"Be straight with me. Are we breaking up?"

"Are you ready to throw in the towel because we see things differently?

"I'm not even sure exactly what we are fighting about. I said I'm sorry. I don't know what more I can do."

"I just want to know if you realize the hoops I went through to have this month with you?"

"Of course I do. Do you know I have walked away from my life for the last ten months? This one week in the last ten months is all I've worked. Sorry it interfered with your time with me. I don't regret doing it. It meant a lot to me to get picked by a person who I admire."

I cannot do this anymore. I'm not going to stand

here and fight with someone over me working. Even though I felt mine and Adler's relationship was going at a slower pace, I thought we were heading in the right direction. I gave him as much of my time as I could this week. He brought me lunch a few times and I stopped what I was doing. I came back to his home every night even though I live closer. I did bend. If he cannot see that, he has blinders on.

I slam his office door on my way out. If he takes it as me throwing in the towel, so be it. He can think whatever he wants, I don't really care at this moment.

I walk into Adler's master bedroom and slam that door shut too. I cross my fingers he doesn't come after me. I need time to think. I have to process everything that was said. That is how I work.

CHAPTER THIRTEEN
ADLER

Well that didn't go so well at all. I went over the conversation I wanted to have with Ciara too many times in my head throughout the day. In my head, it didn't turn into a hot mess. It was just two adults expressing their feelings and moving on. The way she just stormed out of my office, tells me the next two weeks might never come. I hope that's not the case, though. I want us to continue getting to know one another. I think we need to work on communication skills better, but other than that, our relationship has been incredibly wonderful.

I want to go to my room and demand we work this out right this second. The logical part of me knows we need to regroup before we try to have another conversation. Working things out while tempers are high, doesn't solve problems. It tends to make things worse. I do know when we do talk, she needs to know, I see no flaws in her. I won't be able to express that enough, I feel. My words did come out wrong. I am human after all.

I leave my office, I already know Ciara is in my bedroom. It wasn't hard to miss the sound of the door being slammed. I grab my keys off the kitchen island and walk out of the door. I need some fresh air and maybe a run to help clear my mind.

The weather is the perfect temperature to be outside. Too bad I am not enjoying this nice evening with Ciara. I would much rather have her walking with me with her hand in mine, than be walking alone. Even if we didn't talk. Ciara and I have had quiet evenings. Sometimes, it's just nice to have someone next to you. There is a sense of security from having a person you can't get anywhere else.

I walk as far as the park, then I break into a jog. I keep running faster and faster until my lungs are burning. I stop to catch my breath for only a moment before I start running back. When I'm just about halfway back, I slow my pace to a walk. Running didn't do me any good. I still feel like shit for how mine and Ciara's conversation went. I don't think I will feel any better until we have a real conversation without defenses getting the best of us.

When I reached my condo building, I took one

look and kept on walking. If I know Ciara like I think I do, she won't be coming out of my room any time soon. She is the type of person who needs to think everything through. If I go back inside, I might not give her the time that she needs.

As I walked around, I stopped off at a deli and bought a couple of sandwiches. I remember a few days ago when I took Ciara lunch that she loved the grilled chicken panini. She slept the entire day away, so she's got to be hungry. If she hasn't come out of the bedroom yet, I hope she will at least eat. Walking around gave me more time to think about what I need to say to Ciara. I am hoping this time I don't screw up my words.

When I walk into my condo, I see Ciara down the hall coming out of my room. She stops in her tracks when she sees me. I hold up the bag from the deli. She smiles.

"I took the liberty of getting you one of those grilled chicken panini sandwiches."

"I was wondering where you disappeared to."

"I took a run, then I walked around for quite some time thinking."

"Did it help? The run?"

"I think it did." she looks at the bag. *"I'll get us some plates."*

I get plates out, then open the bag, taking the sandwiches out. When I unwrap them and place hers on a plate, I slide it over to her.

"Thank you. I am so hungry."

I put mine on my plate and then sit down next to her. I am hungry too, but I can't eat. The vibe between Ciara and I has definitely changed. I feel it more than I did before we blew up at one another. I don't know if this relationship is going to go much further.

"I am going back to Kentucky."

"When?"

"I am going to call my pilot first thing in the morning."

Ciara pushes her plate away and twists in her seat to face me. *"I noticed you said you are going back to Kentucky."*

"I know you feel the change in us as I do." I push my plate away and run my hands down my face. *"Ciara, I adore you more than anyone I have ever been with. I said things earlier that didn't come out right at all. I see no flaws in you. Maybe the flaws lay within me. I've been an asshole about the canceled*

dinner plans and not coming to be by your side at Asher and Cora's home. I upset you and I don't like it."

"I was an asshole, too, so don't you dare try taking full blame."

"Let's be real with each other, okay." she nods her head. *"Do you see yourself falling in love with me?"*

"I think you are a very sweet, kind man, Alder. Our relationship is going slower than some of the other ones I've had. We definitely have sexual chemistry."

"Sex is important, but there are other things that build a strong relationship. One of them is communication. I get that couple's fight and become stronger because of it. Something has shifted with us. I felt it as soon as I walked in. I would walk across hot coals for you if I knew you felt the same way about me."

"Are you in love with me?"

"I am. You have everything I would want in a woman. Because I am in love with you, I became a jerk. I just wanted to spend all my time with you. It's like I can't get enough of you."

Ciara gets up from the kitchen island. She walks around to the other side. Her eyes connect with mine. I see the tears building. I want to go to her and hold her in my embrace.

"I like you a lot, Adler. I just don't know if I will get to the point where you are in the next two weeks. I don't want to hurt you. I care about you too much."

Her tears drip from the bottom lids of her eyes. My eyes tear up, as well. I lost the girl that made me feel more than anyone ever has. My dream girl just slipped out of my reach and there's no getting her back. It fucking hurts. I get up from my spot and pull her into my arms.

"I have no regrets. Meeting you has been the time of my life."

"There is no time stamp on love. I read that in one of your books while you were gone."

"You can stay here tonight or go home. The choice is yours."

"I think it might be best if I go."

"Ya, you are probably right."

I kiss her cheek then walk away. I grab my keys and walk out of my condo. There is no way I can watch her walk out of my life. I wish her the very best, I really do. I hope all her dreams are fulfilled. She deserves the very best that life has to offer.

CHAPTER FOURTEEN
CIARA

My eyes are full of tears. What in the world just happened? How did mine and Adler's relationship crumble so fast after it was slowly moving forward? I don't understand how we got here. Even though my eyes are filled with tears, I think this is the right thing to do. I have no true way of knowing if my feelings for Adler would have developed into something more real or even if we would have gotten over this hurdle we just had. Adler is right, I felt the shift in our relationship. It wasn't a good shift, either. I keep wiping my face as I pack my bags. I guess I am finding my own way home since he left.

I bring my stuff to the front door and set it down. I get out my phone to send Porter a text asking him to come and pick me up. As I wait, I go to Adler's home office and sit behind his desk. I open his notebook and begin to write.

Adler, it has been one of the greatest moments in my life meeting you. I am sorry that we are not the happy ever after love story you were hoping for. I think about the line you wrote in your book about there not being a timestamp on love, I think it's one of the best things I have ever read. Our timing was just at the wrong time.

Going through this process of finding the perfect man for me has taught me my timing may not be set in stone. I know I may have just given up the right person for me. My feelings are all over the place. My heart is in a tangled mess that I may not get the happy ever after love story either. It's a risk worth taking. I didn't know that until today. I hope that love finds you. You truly are a wonderful man. I wish nothing but the best for you. Don't give up on love. I never will. Do me one favor, please finish the book you started with me. I am looking forward to knowing how it ends. Love, Ciara.

I put the pen down and push myself away from the desk. I think I just did something I didn't think I was capable of doing. I officially broke up with someone and it doesn't feel very good. I have always been the one being dumped. Hell, I didn't even really break up with Hunter. Grams did that for me. I feel completely horrible. I don't like hurting anyone. I

CHAPTER 14

know what it's like to be the one hurt. These are the worst pair of shoes to ever wear. Sadly, I know they'll be on my feet for days to come.

I check my phone and I've never been more happy to see that Porter is here for me. I get my bags and take one last look around. Before I open the door, I wipe my eyes and take a deep breath. I walk out with my head held high even though I want to hang it in shame. I don't care if people see me crying. I am hurting and I have every right to show it.

I make my way out of the front entrance of Adler's condo building and Porter is pulled up right out front. He gets out when he notices my bags. We put my things in the trunk then he hugs me. I cry harder on his shoulder. He tells me everything is going to be okay. I wish I knew that to be true. All I can do at this point is hope and pray he is right.

I get my bearings enough that I go to the passenger side of the car. I open the door and happen to look across the street. I see Adler sitting on a bench, watching me. He puts his head down. I get in the car as he gets up, runs a hand through his hair, then walks away. I feel even worse. I hate myself right now.

"How am I supposed to get through this?"

"You will, baby girl, you will."

"I don't think I can."

"You will. Want to know why?"

"Yes, tell me."

"Because you will marry the one man that is meant to be in your life forever. I have a feeling come December you will be standing next to that man saying I do."

"I wish I had your confidence."

"Ciara, you are stronger than you know. Your heart is going to end up in the right hands."

I close my eyes and pray the answers come to me. I pray for what Porter has said. I pray that I can make it through the next month without destroying myself in the process.

"Take me home please. I just want to not think anymore. I want to crawl under the covers and cry myself to sleep in your arms."

"You got it."

I look out the back window as we drive away. I just left a piece of my heart behind. How much of it will I have left to give someone by the time November ends?

ABOUT THE AUTHOR

Thank you so much for taking the time to read Grandma's Silent Auction - October. Word-of-mouth is crucial for any author to succeed. If you enjoyed the book, please leave a review on Amazon. Even if it's just a sentence or two. It would make all the difference and would be very much appreciated. – OXOX Michael James

Michael's Links:

Website: http://michaeljames-author332.bravesites.com/

ALSO BY MICHAEL JAMES

If you enjoyed Grandma's Silent Auction - October, you may also like my other books:

The Way We Love series:

Pink Skies At Night

Shadows At Night

Nights Are Unlimited

Concealed By The Night

Shattered At Night

Freed At Night

Winning A Cowgirl's Heart - Trilogy:

The Rodeo King

The Best Friend

The Fate Of My Heart

Winning a Cowgirl's Heart -Complete Box Set

Construction Vs. Corporate- Trilogy:

Unbalanced

Balancing

Balanced

Secrets Within a Club

Club Comrade

Revenge

Saving Club Conrad

Masquerade Saga

His Pearls

His Secrets

His Prison

His Games

His Moves

All His

Crime in Landkaster series

The Mirror

Times Like These

Lonely Road of Faith

Grandma's Silent Auction series

January

February

March

April

May

June

July

August

September

Lost Love Letter

I'll be Waiting

Before I Do

Standalone:

Toying With October

Pieces Of Me

A Christmas For Eve

Dom Diaries: Tangled Up In You

Christmas Scavenger Hunt

Blue Christmas

Stealing the Christmas Spotlight

Co-written with Jodi Fahey

Last Sheet

Co-written with Daniel Grayson

Inside the Storm

Manufactured by Amazon.ca
Bolton, ON